TASK FORCE DELTA
KILL OR CAPTURE

Craig Simpson

EDGE
FRANKLIN WATTS

LONDON•SYDNEY

First published in 2012
by Franklin Watts

Text © Craig Simpson 2012
Illustrations by David Cousens © Franklin Watts 2012
Cover design by Peter Scoulding

Franklin Watts
338 Euston Road
London NW1 3BH

Franklin Watts Australia
Level 17/207 Kent Street
Sydney, NSW 2000

Task Force Delta is a work of fiction. Any resemblance of characters to
persons living or dead is entirely coincidental and unintended and all
statements purporting to be facts are not necessarily true.

A CIP catalogue record for this book
is available from the British Library.

ISBN: 978 1 4451 0697 7

1 3 5 7 9 10 8 6 4 2

Printed in Great Britain

Franklin Watts is a division of Hachette Children's Books,
an Hachette UK company.
www.hachette.co.uk

The Real Delta Force

Task Force Delta is inspired by one
of the United States' top-level secret
military units, the 1st Special Forces
Operational Detachment — Delta (1SFOD-D)

also known as

Delta Force

Delta Force's main missions are direct, counter-terrorism
action. They also carry out many secret assignments
including hostage rescues and raids behind enemy lines.

Delta Force (also called "The Unit")
is based at Fort Bragg, Carolina, USA.

Delta Force's motto is:
"Surprise, Speed, Success"

Major Nathan Connor
Highly decorated
Commander of Delta Force.
Transferred from the 75th
Ranger Regiment. Speaks
five languages including
Pashto.

Lieutenant Danny Crow
Second in command.
Came top of his class in Special Forces'
"Operative Training Course".

Lieutenant Jacko Alvarez
A former Navy Seal and
weapons expert.

Sergeant Major Sparks
Comms and intel expert and
veteran of several Special
Forces units before being hand-
picked for Delta Force.

**Master Sergeant
Ben Saunders**
Transferred from 75th
Ranger Regiment. An
expert in survival skills
and demolition.

**Sergeant First Class
Sam Wilson**
World-class sniper skills led to
recruitment into Delta Force,
despite being just 19 (usual
minimum age 21).

CONTENTS

CHAPTER ONE
Jabir escapes

Kandahar Prison, Afghanistan

The giant wolf spider was the size of a man's hand and very, very fast. In the darkness it scurried over the floor of the prison cell and climbed onto Jabir's outstretched arm. When it ran across his face, he awoke with a start and cried out. He shot bolt upright and frantically slapped his cheeks until certain it was gone.

"Curse these Americans for keeping me in this prison," the elderly Taliban commander whispered, smoothing down his beard. He gazed into the darkness. "But revenge will taste as sweet as honey."

Jabir imagined the flash of his sword as it sliced off the heads of his enemies. It was the same vision he had nearly every night, and he never grew tired of it. The face of one of his enemies was particularly clear; the man who'd taken him prisoner — Major Nathan Connor. "One day, *inshallah*," he muttered. "One day soon, major."

And then Jabir heard something: a curiously dull, rhythmic tapping. It came from beneath the floor. He knelt and pressed an ear against the concrete. He heard it again. "Ibrahim, wake up," he whispered to his slumbering cellmate. He reached out and shook him. "Wake up! Our brothers are coming."

Curled up on the floor, Ibrahim stirred and rubbed the sleep from his eyes.

The tapping grew louder. A crack appeared in the floor. Jabir could see lamplight from the tunnel beyond. The hole widened. Eventually, a dirt-covered face emerged.

"*Assalam u alaikum.* Peace be upon you, Uncle Jabir." The teenage boy climbed up and held out his arms triumphantly.

"It's good to see you, Shafiq." They embraced and bumped shoulders, greeting the Afghan way.

Shafiq was followed by three men, all Taliban, all armed with AK-47s and grenades. "We've dug from the canning factory and under the main road, uncle. We have worked day and night for months. We have infiltrated the guards, too. Some have been bribed, others given a sleeping draught. We plan to get everyone out."

"You have done well."

"Everything is arranged. My father, Faisal, and the others await you. They have clean clothes and transport. By sunrise you will be far away from here. Others will make for the old town. There they shall cause much trouble when the Afghan army and Americans come for them. They know that they are to seize two hostages and bring them to you. I will stay to make sure everything goes to plan. It will be just as you asked, Uncle Jabir. Now, go."

Jabir peered down into the tunnel and listened to the hum of the electric fans needed to maintain a supply of breathable air. He climbed down the rickety, makeshift ladder into the tunnel, with Ibrahim close behind. Now he was a free man, he could lead his men once more. The Taliban would rise up, stronger. Prisoners were loyal to his jihad, his Holy War, and would greatly swell his ranks.

The men crawled on all fours. "Soon the stinking gutters of this crowded city will run red with the blood of the infidel," the Taliban leader muttered.

"Yes, Jabir, and soon the country will be rocked by your masterful and deadly plan."

CHAPTER TWO
Connor's call

Camp Delta

In his tented quarters at Camp Delta, General Patterson, the head of ISAF's Central Command (CENTCOM), had just soaped up his chin and begun shaving with his cut-throat razor when a sergeant burst in. "Sir?"

"Arrgh! Goddamnit!" Blood trickled down Patterson's neck. He flung the razor down and spun round. "What?"

The sergeant explained that he'd just received news of the mass prison break-out.

Patterson wiped away the blood and suds with the towel draped about his neck and bellowed, "How many?"

"Three hundred and forty-seven, sir. Including the Taliban commander, Jabir Hassani."

"Hassani. Jeeezzzusss!" Tightness gripped the general's chest as he recalled Jabir's ruthlessness, the years it had taken to capture him, and the lives of many good men it had cost.

"Roadblocks have been set up around Kandahar, sir. According to reports, many escapees have headed into the old town. The

Afghan National Army have Colonel Khalid on the ground there. He intends searching house-to-house."

Patterson stared at his reflection in the small, cracked shaving mirror, and groaned. He'd suddenly aged a decade. Colonel Khalid was on first-name terms with the Afghan president. Worse, he was fuelled by ambition. Despite being a fine soldier, it made him reckless and dangerous. Patterson knew on this occasion Khalid was out of his depth. The local garrison of ANA recruits under Khalid's command wasn't yet ready to undertake such a major operation. Their training was patchy, and they'd only ever managed to weed out a handful of Taliban sympathisers. Patterson closed his eyes and cursed. "Sergeant, we're going to have to intervene with a show of force. Get Alpha and Bravo Company off their butts and ready to move out in one hour. Call Khalid and request that he secure the area, but not to start the search until our guys arrive to support him. And tell Major Connor I want to see him, now."

"Yes, general."

"Delta's skills may be called upon. And Connor understands the way Jabir thinks."

CHAPTER THREE
Into the old town

Kandahar's old town

Mid-morning, Major Nathan Connor and his team arrived in their modified GMV at the outskirts of Kandahar's old town. It was chaos. Dozens of armoured vehicles were parked up close together. Groups of ANA soldiers stood around at road junctions, while others pulled razor wire across the road to form a barricade. Black Hawk helicopters roared overhead, circling at low altitude. In the searing heat, dozens of US marines in body armour and full kit were standing around clutching their weapons, sweating and waiting nervously to move out; others were running to and fro as final preparations were made. General Patterson's parting orders rang in Connor's ears — find Jabir and this time I don't give a damn whether you kill or capture him! Connor jumped out of the GMV and headed over to Sergeant Baxter from Alpha Company, US Marines, who was holding a map and yelling orders.

"What's happening?" asked Connor.

Baxter saluted. "Major, we're preparing to go in. All platoon leaders have been issued with hand-held fingerprint scanners linked to the ISAF prisoner database. Our orders are to check every adult male. If they're in there, we'll find them."

Nodding, Connor snatched the map and studied it. The ancient old town occupied a rectangle covering over a square kilometre. The area was divided by four main streets converging at a central square. Low-rise brick and concrete houses were crammed in with shops and bazaars.

"Where's Colonel Khalid?" Connor asked Baxter.

The sergeant shrugged. "Not seen him, sir. I'd heard he's already gone in with a small ANA team. Something about receiving a tip-off and wanting his unit to have the glory of recapturing Jabir Hassani themselves."

"Just like Khalid," Connor muttered. "It's bound to be a trap. Jabir's no fool. I figure he'll be long gone by now. OK, carry on. But when you move out, for God's sake keep your wits about you and make sure CENTCOM gives you constant aerial updates from our drones."

"Yes, sir." Baxter strode off, got his men into line, and then moved beyond the barricade.

While travelling into town from Camp Delta, Connor had texted some of his contacts, unscrupulous shopkeepers in the bazaar who sold the most precious and expensive of goods — information. Replies confirmed his suspicions that Jabir had most likely fled the city. But to where? None of his contacts knew. Connor had only one option left — to hang around in the hope that Baxter located one of Jabir's men who might have the answers they needed.

Connor returned to his GMV and climbed into the front passenger seat. He took a swig of water from a bottle as Baxter's men left the first building empty-handed.

Lieutenant Jacko Alvarez rested his arms on the steering wheel and groaned resignedly. "Major, I think we're in for a long day."

Connor nodded. "Sparks, see if you can get hold of Colonel Khalid on the radio. I think he's hellbent on becoming a hero."

"Yes, sir."

A deafening explosion rocked the street. Jacko leaned forward and gazed straight ahead at the cloud of smoke rising over the old town. "Quite possibly a dead hero, sir."

"That's what's worrying me. Sparks, any luck?"

"I'm through, sir," Sergeant Sparks announced from the back of the vehicle. "Khalid's alive and in the central square. A car bomb's taken out four of his men and the rest are pinned down by Taliban snipers. His personnel carrier's out of action, too. Took a hit from an RPG. I'll get CENTCOM to patch through a visual feed to us."

Connor and his team studied the small screen on Spark's comms gear. Amid rising, acrid smoke from burning vehicles they could see Khalid and two of his men crouching behind a low wall.

"Hell! There's no time to mess around. We'd better go get them." Connor leaned out and yelled at a sentry. "Move that wire barricade, marine."

"I have a bad feeling about this, sir," said Jacko as he started up their GMV. "We could be walking into a trap as well. We all heard Jabir Hassani swear he'd get his revenge against us that day we captured him."

"Just drive, lieutenant... Danny, you're up top. Point that M2 at anything that breathes... Sparks, tell Khalid to sit tight. And see if you can get air support to lay down some suppressing fire around the square. Those snipers need distracting... Ben and Sam, keep your eyes peeled. Knowing Jabir's men, I bet these streets are littered with IEDs." Connor swung round his M4 carbine and released the safety catch. "OK, guys, time to go hunting."

CHAPTER FOUR
IED strike

Jacko drove steadily for the first fifty metres, but hit the brakes when Connor raised his hand. Baxter was emerging from a building. He gave Connor the thumbs up as an escapee with his hands cuffed behind his back was dragged out of the doorway. "Three hundred and forty-six to go, major."

"Hey, Baxter, want to see some real action?" Connor shouted.

"Yes siree, major, sir." Baxter grinned.

Connor quickly briefed him. "So, you and your men secure this street and follow us towards the square. You're our backup, sergeant. This is going to be our exit route. Maintain radio contact with us at all times. Getting Colonel Khalid out of here isn't going to be easy."

Connor instructed Jacko to edge forward slowly. Sporadic small arms fire could be heard coming from the square ahead. But that wasn't what worried Connor most. It was the eyes staring at him that gave him a sinking feeling; eyes peering out of windows, eyes of men in the street, on balconies, on bicycles and mopeds. Who was friend and who was foe? It was impossible to tell.

Danny aimed the GMV's swivelled, top-mounted M2 machine gun threateningly at anyone who came too close. He yelled at them to back off. This wasn't the time for winning hearts and minds. Any one of them could be a suicide bomber.

Sam spotted him first. "Man on balcony to our right holding a mobile phone, sir."

"Goddamnit, major, he's got an accomplice, too," Ben added. "On the roof. He's carrying a camcorder."

Connor understood — a bomb was waiting for them, to be detonated remotely by phone signal. The horror would be captured on video and no doubt uploaded to extremist websites. But, where was the bomb? His eyes darted left then right, before settling on a battered old truck parked up some forty metres ahead. If it was packed with explosives, they were in big trouble.

"Jacko, back up. Now!"

They had to move fast or else risk becoming prime time news. Jacko slammed the GMV into reverse.

"Oh, Jeeesus! The guy's started dialling!" Sam shouted. "Get a move on."

With the GMV lurching backwards, Connor made a snap decision. "Danny, take them out."

It was too late. The bomb detonated, blasting

debris high into the sky. The force lifted the GMV a metre into the air, flipping it onto its side. Danny's grip on the M2 machine gun was torn and he was flung clear. A red-hot and razor-sharp piece of shrapnel cut across his face as he tumbled heavily onto the roadside. More shrapnel peppered the GMV, as Connor and his men were thrown around inside.

A dust cloud crept along the street amid an eerie silence. The twisted bodies of innocent civilians lay still in the road.

"Major? Major Connor, sir? Are you OK?"

CHAPTER FIVE
Race to the square

Connor's ears rang. He felt light-headed. He opened his eyes and Baxter's concerned face gradually came into focus. Connor grabbed Baxter's outstretched hand and managed to scramble out. Sam and Ben crawled out of the back of the vehicle. Sparks followed, spitting out two teeth dislodged by Ben's elbow. A winded Danny rose to his feet and wiped away the blood oozing from the deep cut across his face. Shrapnel lodged in his battle fatigues started to smoke and burn his skin. Hurriedly, he yanked the pieces out.

Baxter's men helped extract Jacko from behind the steering wheel. "Jeesh, you guys had one hell of a lucky escape. Shall we fall back, major?"

Connor adjusted his helmet and took a deep breath. Gunfire could still be heard coming from the square. Colonel Khalid still needed rescuing. "No, sergeant." He looked at the houses lining the street, all single-storey, all flat roofed. "Time for Plan B. You clear a path on the road, we'll get to the square via the rooftops."

Baxter hesitated. "Listen, major, it ain't our

guys in trouble, sir. Why can't the ANA troops have a go?"

"Experience is going to count here, sergeant. Khalid isn't just any old ANA commander either. He has the ear of the Afghan president and is extremely influential. He's a useful bridge between ISAF and the government. Letting him get killed won't look good. Rescuing him alive, on the other hand, will earn us top marks."

The sergeant nodded. "All right then, major."

"Sparks," Connor called out, "warn those

Black Hawks that we'll be on the roofs. Friendly fire is the last thing we need."

"Yes, sir."

Connor gritted his teeth. "Right. Let's do it."

Delta Force moved swiftly across the flat rooftops and terraces in three pairs, Danny and Jacko leading the way. They pushed their way between the washing hanging on lines, using low parapet walls for cover. The sun beat down on Connor and his men. Everywhere they looked the air shimmered from the rising heat. Flies buzzed about their faces. It was easily 35 degrees Celsius. Connor kept one eye on Baxter's progress below. Already the marines had managed to make good headway and were closer to the square, with Baxter out in front. Suddenly Jacko dropped to one knee and held up his left hand. Connor froze.

Jacko lay down and crawled to the next parapet and risked glancing over. He saw four armed Taliban below, crouching in the shade of a walled backyard and busily loading their AK-47s. Two women in black burqas were preparing bread dough. A clutch of young children were making kites out of plastic bags and string. Shimmying backwards out of sight, he signalled to the rest of the team. Connor ordered the others to fan out along the rooftop. He couldn't risk moving past.

They had to be dealt with. He signalled to Jacko and Danny.

They leapt to their feet. With the element of surprise, a short burst of rapid fire from their silenced M4 carbines dealt with the four armed insurgents, stray bullets punching out chunks of the yard's wall. The women screamed. They grabbed up their children and ran indoors. Danny and Jacko hurriedly jumped down into the yard, Danny covering the open door while Jacko readied to search inside. He switched on his M4's rail-mounted tactical light and visible laser marker. Cautiously, his pulse racing as the adrenaline surged, he stepped through the doorway. He supressed the fear — of enemies waiting in the dark — and swept the room. The narrow circle of light picked out furniture and cast weird shadows. Nothing. He breathed a sigh of relief. "Clear," he whispered into his mic.

Danny joined him and they targeted another open door. Jacko edged forward and aimed through it. The next room was darker still. Heart in his mouth, finger on trigger, he stepped through. Rapidly sweeping the room, the beam of light fell upon a huddle of frightened faces in one corner — the women and children. Then it lit a pile of cushions. They moved. Jacko saw the barrel of an AK-47 emerge and he let rip. The cushions danced as stuffing flew out from the bullet holes. A Taliban fighter groaned and rolled out from among them. "Clear!" Jacko shouted.

"Get back up here," Connor responded. "We've got more trouble."

A Taliban sniper was spotted on a distant rooftop. He held his rifle up to his shoulder, ready to fire on Baxter's marines when they moved into his field of fire. Sam pulled his M110A1 semi-automatic sniper rifle tightly to his shoulder, took aim and fired. The crouching Taliban sniper fell forward and dropped over the parapet to the street below. Sam's feeling of satisfaction was short-lived.

"Incoming RPG from top of mosque minaret," Ben yelled, dropping flat.

Connor saw it too, but quickly realised it was Baxter's men being targeted. The RPG hit a building opposite. The blast collapsed a wall down onto several of the men below. Seconds later he heard Baxter over the radio shout frantically, "Man down! Man down! Bring in the heavy armour now. Need urgent casualty evac."

As the dust cleared, Connor could just make out Baxter pulling a marine from beneath the rubble.

With Jacko and Danny rejoining the others on the roof, they concentrated fire on the minaret until certain the Taliban with the RPG had been taken out. Connor decided to make a dash over the remaining forty metres to the square. Reaching for a smoke grenade, he activated it and threw it so it spun through the air discharging a broad yellowish cloud of dense smoke. Connor led the team forwards, ducking under clothes lines, knocking aside old plastic chairs and jumping over stone parapets. They fired at insurgents on the surrounding rooftops as they moved until they finally reached the roof overlooking the square. Crouching and hurriedly reloading, they took in the scene below.

"What the hell...?" Ben exclaimed as he smacked in a fresh ammo magazine.

Connor was struck by it too. Although a pall of smoke from burnt-out vehicles hung over the square, he could see six bodies in ANA uniform. None resembled Khalid. The square was utterly deserted. Even the Taliban snipers seemed to have melted away. The scene felt unreal.

"Sparks, try raising Colonel Khalid on the radio."

"Yes, sir."

"Baxter, where are you?" Connor shouted into his helmet microphone. "I can't see you or any of your men. Baxter... Come in, Baxter, over."

"Sir, Khalid's not responding," said Sparks.

There was no reply from Baxter either.

Within five minutes the square filled with tanks, armoured personnel carriers and ISAF troops from both Alpha and Bravo Company. The area was quickly sealed off. It took just another five minutes for Connor to realise that Colonel Khalid had vanished, along with Sergeant Baxter.

"We'll find them, sir," said Danny.

"Don't count on it," Connor responded. "I reckon Jabir had this all thought through."

"But why take Khalid and Baxter?"

Connor squinted up at the burning sun.

"That's the million dollar question. What exactly is Jabir up to? Somehow, I have a horrible feeling this is just the beginning."

CHAPTER SIX
Jabir's hostages

Arghandab valley, north-west of Kandahar

Deep in the Arghandab valley north-west of Kandahar, between the Loy Wiyala canal and Arghandab River, a battered old Lexus saloon rumbled along a stony track leading to the remote village. Either side lay pomegranate and grape orchards laden with ripening fruit, and fields of wheat and poppies crisscrossed by irrigation channels and wadis. The Lexus pulled into a walled compound and stopped. Two ANA soldiers climbed out of the front and Jabir's nephew, Shafiq, from the back. They were greeted by a tall, slim man emerging from the house; Jabir's brother, Faisal.

"We did it, Father," Shafiq declared. "Come!"

Running to the back of the car, Shafiq opened the boot. Inside lay Colonel Khalid and Sergeant Baxter, their mouths taped, their heads hooded, their wrists and ankles bound.

Faisal peered into the boot and grinned with delight. "Allah be praised, Shafiq, once again you have proven yourself to be worthy of our cause." More Taliban emerged from the building and he issued instructions. "Take the prisoners to see Jabir."

While Khalid and Baxter were manhandled from the boot and dragged indoors, Faisal turned to the two ANA soldiers. "I trust you weren't followed." They shook their heads. "Good. Come with me. I will get the money you are owed." He led them into an outbuilding, drew his pistol and shot them both at point-blank range.

Shafiq had followed on his father's heels and was shocked by what he saw. "But they were loyal to our cause."

"True, but they knew too much. We couldn't risk them betraying us. They are martyrs, Shafiq. Now, I must join the others. I'll leave you to burn the bodies and dispose of the car."

Inside the farmhouse, Khalid and Baxter were dragged in front of Jabir, who was reclining on a pile of cushions and eating chunks of bread he'd dipped into a bowl of shorwa: a thin, oily broth. He licked his fingers before signalling for their hoods to be removed and the tape covering their mouths to be ripped free.

Shaken and disorientated, both Colonel Khalid and Sergeant Baxter were unsteady on their feet.

"You'll pay for this, Hassani," Baxter snarled defiantly, struggling to tear his bindings loose.

Ibrahim slammed the butt of his AK-47 into Baxter's back. The sergeant crashed to his knees.

Jabir popped a juicy grape into his mouth, chewed a moment, and then spoke. "Welcome to my humble home. I trust your journey was... uncomfortable."

"What do you intend doing with us?" asked Khalid fearfully.

Jabir called out, and moments later a burly Taliban fighter entered the room clutching an impressive, ornate sword. Jabir rose to his feet and took the sword. He touched the curved blade to the colonel's exposed neck. Khalid froze.

"It is very simple," Jabir sneered. "I have a list of demands. You shall read them out. We will video you. ISAF and the Afghan government will have one week to comply."

"Or?" Khalid dared ask.

Jabir moved forward, the sword blade nicking Khalid's neck. The colonel gasped. But the tip struck the wall behind him, skewering a wolf spider that had the misfortune of being in the wrong place at the right time. "Or else you will both die!" Jabir warned.

CHAPTER SEVEN
Rescue mission

Camp Delta

General Patterson was in the Ops Room at Camp
Delta. With him were Major Connor and two men
from CENTCOM's Intelligence Unit. They were
huddled round a laptop viewing Jabir's video
again. It had been widely distributed to the media
and posted on YouTube. The whole world knew
about it. Millions had seen Khalid and Baxter on
their knees, reading out the demands. Jabir stood
over them, his sword held above their heads.

Patterson turned away and paced the room.
The heat was getting to him. Jabir's demands
were impossible to meet. "It's ridiculous!
Jabir's mad. He wants all foreign troops out
of Afghanistan. He wants all Taliban prisoners
released from prisons in Kabul and Lashkar Gah,
and the return of all detainees at Guantanamo."
He turned to one of the intel guys, Lieutenant
Sharp. "You said you had some good news?"

"Yes, sir. We believe some rogue ANA helped
the Taliban get Khalid and Baxter out of the
old town. Two have gone AWOL. Routine drone
reconnaissance feeds recorded a vehicle

containing two ANA and a youth heading west into the Arghandab valley. They passed unchallenged through a checkpoint manned by other ANA who have since been arrested and are undergoing questioning. Also, we believe Jabir Hassani has made a fatal error. We've traced the location where the video was uploaded from. It's in the same valley. A compound at a remote farming village. We've briefed Major Connor and he's come up with a plan."

"Well?" Patterson eyeballed Connor. "Can we get them out alive? The Afghan president insists we do everything we can, or else there will be dire consequences."

Connor inspected a detailed map on the wall of the Ops Room. "This is where we think they're being held, sir." He pointed.

Full of impatience, Patterson interrupted. "Right, Delta Force can helo at night and kick some butt. Just tell me what you need, major."

Connor shook his head. "No, sir. That's precisely what Jabir will expect. He'll hear us coming and kill the hostages — assuming, of course, they're still alive. Jabir's not prone to making mistakes... like revealing his whereabouts by letting us trace the location they accessed the Internet from. Unless..."

Patterson frowned. "I don't understand. What are you saying?"

"Unless it was deliberate, sir. Jabir wants us to know the location. He'll expect us to attempt a rescue. It'll be a trap."

Patterson's shoulders sagged. "Then what do you suggest?"

"The Canadians have a small Forward Operating Base five kilometres from the target, sir, FOB Crossbow. They've been having a rough time lately with Taliban snipers and nightly

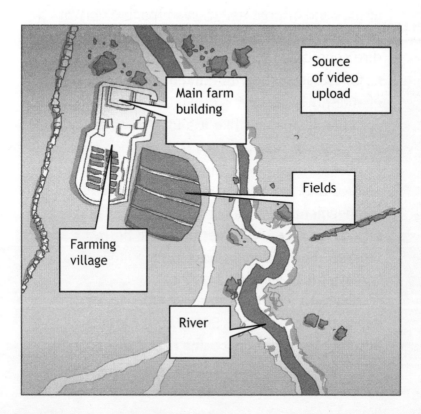

incoming mortar fire. I've spoken to their commander and he tells me that they control barely a kilometre in any direction. Venture any further and they get attacked, and the area is littered with IEDs. If we launched an assault from there on foot, again we'd quickly run into trouble. However, they are close to the river. That's the key, sir. I've broken the mission down into stages. From FOB Crossbow we carry lightweight collapsible canoes to the river. The guys from Crossbow are willing to clear our route of IEDs and insurgents. Then we paddle upriver to a location just a few hundred metres from the farming village. From there we go in silently, and hard. With the cover of darkness we'll retain the element of surprise."

"I like it, major, I like it a lot. How quickly can your team be ready to move?"

"Twenty-four hours, sir. Lieutenants Alvarez and Crow are making the necessary arrangements. We'll have air support available to pick us up once the target area and hostages are secured. But..." Connor hesitated.

"What is it, major?"

"I reckon Jabir's up to something. There has to be more to this. Either he'll move the hostages or he's simply using it as a diversion for something else." Connor turned to the men from Intelligence. "Is there anything I should know about? Anything supposedly being kept secret?"

"No, sir. Except, well, I'm not sure it's important."

"What?"

"The Afghan president is scheduled to make a visit to the area the day after tomorrow. It's the official opening of a major new section of canal and irrigation network beneath the Dhala dam. He's going to make a keynote speech about how big construction projects can improve the lives of ordinary Afghans."

"Goddamnit, that's it!" Connor felt like he'd just solved a really tricky crossword puzzle. "That's Jabir's real target; the Afghan president. You must cancel the visit — but cancel it right at the last moment so as not to alert Jabir that we're onto him. And send in overwhelming force. You mustn't let Jabir slip through your net."

General Patterson grimaced. "Impossible. The Afghan president won't cancel. He always refuses to show weakness, and there are elections looming. We'll just have to try to keep him safe. Leave that to us, major. We'll find a way. I need you to concentrate on rescuing Khalid and Baxter. Don't let me down, major."

CHAPTER EIGHT
Delta close in

Forward Operating Base Crossbow

FOB Crossbow was little more than a square of parched earth surrounded by razor wire, HESCO fortifications, sandbags and twin towers housing mortars and machine guns. Hitching a lift on a Cobra helo, Delta Force touched down an hour before dusk and offloaded their gear. Connor was met by the base commander, Captain Lee Walsh.

"Welcome to Crossbow, major. It's a bit rough and ready, but I'm sure you're used to that. We're pretty isolated up here, so it's nice to see some new faces. Come with me and I'll show you the route we've cleared for your team leading down to the river." Walsh led Connor up one of the towers. "There's a decent view from up here." He handed Connor a pair of binoculars and pointed. "For maximum cover, we stuck to that ditch. It leads to within twenty metres of the river bank. We had to diffuse three IEDs along the way. Privates Jennings and Stokes here have orders to make sure the Taliban don't come back to plant more bombs before you begin your mission."

Jennings was manning the machine gun. He

seemed relaxed, chewing a stick of gum. Stokes was peering through a tripod-mounted ranging scope. In the heat their uniforms were drenched in sweat. "There's been some movement, sir, but every time they come out into the open, we send them running for cover."

"You said you were being attacked almost every night," Connor remarked.

Jennings looked up from his weapon. "Yep, every night for the past month. It's true what they tell us during basic training, sir."

"What is?"

"That soldiering is basically long periods of extreme boredom, followed by short periods of extreme violence, sir." He grinned. "But it's worth the wait!"

Connor raised the binoculars and surveyed the terrain; flat, dusty green, and crisscrossed by shallow ditches and wadis. The ground eventually sloped down to a band of dense undergrowth by the river. He handed the binoculars back. "Thank you, captain. Your efforts are much appreciated. We'll move out at midnight."

Jacko led the men, their faces blackened for camouflage, along the ditch. Behind him Sam, Danny and Ben dragged the three collapsible two-man canoes and paddles. Connor and Sparks brought up the rear. With the moon obscured by cloud, the darkness was almost complete. The stifling heat of the day had been replaced by a cool breeze filled with the frantic chatter of insects and the distant sound of the river. Through their helmet-mounted night-vision aids, their surroundings looked otherworldly — giant moths glowing brightly as they zigzagged through the night air.

Midway along the ditch the calm was shattered by an explosion and distant crack of rifle fire. Connor looked round and saw that FOB Crossbow was under attack. To his relief it appeared that the Taliban had launched their assault from the other direction. Within seconds phosphorous flares arced high into the sky. As their flickering light lit the valley beyond, Private Jennings returned fire from the tower. Connor watched for a minute before turning his back on them. He continued to crawl along the ditch. Almost immediately, he bumped into Sparks, who signalled that voices had been heard up ahead. Connor moved silently along the line and tapped Jacko on the shoulder.

Jacko pointed.

Connor saw two figures heading towards them

on all fours. They had rifles slung across their backs. They were talking to one another and completely oblivious to Delta Force's presence. Connor ran a finger across his throat and drew his knife. Jacko drew his too. They remained perfectly still and waited, watching.

CHAPTER NINE
A nasty surprise

"Khatar day?"

"Hoo."

"Dalta nazhde kum mayn shta?"

"Na — aarr!"

Connor wiped the blood from his knife on the Taliban fighter's clothes. Jacko crawled over the two bodies and continued on a further fifty metres. Then he whispered over the radio that the rest of the ditch was clear. Connor ordered the others to move up.

At the river, they slipped the canoes into the water and set off upriver, hugging the bank for maximum cover. The muscles in their arms began to burn as they pulled against the strong current. They pressed on, desperate to remain silent, desperate to remain unnoticed.

After an hour's exertion, Connor checked his wrist-mounted GPS locator. He was relieved that they'd finally reached his planned point to go ashore. He paddled hard left to take him towards the bank and thick undergrowth. The others followed and they dragged their canoes onto the muddy bank.

Connor needed to get a proper look at the

layout of the village — located about two hundred metres away — before making a move on the compound where intel had placed Jabir, Colonel Khalid and Baxter. He lay flat, using his elbows to haul himself through a stinking irrigation ditch. He emerged from tall spiky grass about fifty metres from the nearest building.

To his left was a pomegranate orchard, to his right a field of wheat. Straight ahead was a stony track leading to the cluster of walled compounds, and several derelict outbuildings. He scanned the whole area with a thermal-imaging scope, but saw no sign of any guards. If any were there, they were well hidden. He radioed for the others to join him.

"Do you reckon they've moved the hostages, sir?" Ben asked. "This place looks deserted."

"Don't know. Guess we'd better find out. Sparks and Sam stay here and cover our exit. Sparks, keep an open channel to CENTCOM and make sure air support is ready to come and evac us at a moment's notice. Ben and Danny — you're Team Two — enter via the back of the compound and get onto the flat roof of the target building as quickly as possible. Standard protocol; clear the first floor while Jacko and I deal with the ground level. Move in on my command. Good luck, guys."

Delta Force moved swiftly and silently from one place of cover to the next. Connor and Jacko entered the field of wheat and reached part of the compound's mud-brick wall that had collapsed. They waited, crouching in the dark. A click in Connor's ear was followed by Danny's voice. Team Two had arrived at the rear of the compound. "Roger that. Go!" Connor replied.

Jacko was first over the wall. On the other side he knelt and swept the compound with his M4. Once over, Connor ran towards a side door in the farmhouse. He noticed the windows had been blacked out. The only sound was the whirr and clatter of an electricity generator in a nearby outhouse. Danny and Ben appeared on the top of the wall at the rear of the compound. They ran along it, stooping to maintain their balance as it rose up a good three metres. When close enough to the farmhouse, they jumped onto the flat roof and prepared to enter through a first-floor window. "Team Two in position, over."

Connor checked the doorframe closely for signs of a booby trap, but there was nothing suspicious. He gave the order to enter.

Ben forced in the window on the first floor and Danny scanned the room. It was clear. Ben quickly climbed through and they began to check the upstairs rooms. At the same time, Jacko entered the dark hallway, crouched down and waved Connor forward. Through their night-vision gear they could see the hallway was empty.

"Clear! ... Clear! ... Clear!" It all happened in seconds; crashing doors as they got kicked open, shouting as Danny and Ben checked the upstairs rooms. Jacko and Connor moved fast too, each taking rooms on opposite sides of the hall.

"Clear!" Connor shouted.

"Oh, Jeezzuss! In here, major."

Connor turned and hurried across the hallway, entering a sparsely furnished room. To his right a TV and DVD player stood on a large box. To his left, Colonel Khalid and Sergeant Baxter were sitting on the floor, propped up against the wall, their decapitated heads resting in their laps.

Suddenly, the TV burst into life.

Startled and unnerved Connor and Jacko spun round. "What the...?"

The TV picture showed Jabir Hassani sitting cross-legged. A cheap motion sensor had been rigged to the DVD player's "on" switch, triggering the video to start when someone entered the room.

"First floor secure," Danny said over the radio.

"I don't like this," Connor snapped, staring at Khalid and Baxter.

Jabir raised a hand, almost as if waving, and began to speak. "So, we meet again Major Connor."

"How the...?" Jacko's jaw dropped.

"Sparks! Sam! We've been set up. Watch for movement," Connor barked.

Jabir leaned forward towards the camera lens and continued. "My sources informed me that Delta Force had been assigned with the rescue attempt. As you can see, I'm afraid you are too late, major. You should have killed me when you had the chance, but you didn't. And tomorrow the president will die too, major. Of course, I know you'll try to stop me and you'll try to protect him. But you will FAIL!"

"We're leaving. Now!" Connor shouted. "Team Two fall back to your entry point."

On the TV, Jabir continued but no one was watching. He began ranting, repeating his demands, spitting hatred at all non-believers, raging that his Taliban would be victorious in their jihad.

Connor and Jacko were halfway across the compound when the bomb linked to the DVD player detonated. The explosion flung them to the ground.

A few hundred metres away, Shafiq crouched behind a dry-stone wall separating two fields of poppies overlooking the compound. He had been watching events unfold through a pair of night-vision binoculars his father had stolen from the ANA. He'd seen soldiers enter. He'd watched the building explode. And now he could hear the rhythmic thwack-thwack of helicopter rotors in the distance. He took his mobile phone from his pocket and dialled.

"Uncle Jabir, you were right. They did come. The bomb's exploded but I think they got out alive. Their helicopters are coming for them."

Jabir laughed. "No matter. They have been deceived. It is enough of a victory for one day. Tomorrow, they shall all die. Well done, Shafiq. Come and join us. We shall watch them die together."

Shafiq put the phone back into his pocket and leapt over the wall. Clambering onto his dirt bike, he kick-started it and gunned the throttle. The buzz of the two-stroke engine echoed through the valley. He switched on the headlamp and headed north, tyres kicking dust. He was looking forward to tomorrow. His uncle's plan would make headline news around the world. Jabir Hassani would be famous. And he, young Shafiq, had played his part. He felt proud. But as he tore up a rough trail, something bothered him. Despite being certain he'd followed his uncle's orders precisely, deep down he had the feeling he'd forgotten to do something; something important.

CHAPTER TEN
Connor works it out

Camp Delta

"There's a leak. Jabir knew we were assigned to the rescue mission, general," Connor complained angrily. "Either he's able to intercept our comms traffic, or some of those ANA who wander in and out of Camp Delta are passing on information."

General Patterson squirmed in his chair. "We'll tighten security."

"A bit late for that! And you say the president's read my report but still insists on delivering his speech this evening. Does he want to die? He's crazy. Why can't he make his speech from somewhere else, somewhere safe?"

Unable to offer an explanation, Patterson shrugged. "At least he's agreed to wear body armour, and he'll be surrounded by both our guys and his most trusted bodyguards. Press access is restricted, and we'll have drones and snipers covering the whole area. When the time comes we'll also jam all mobile phone signals for a radius of three kilometres, so there's no chance of remote detonation of a hidden bomb."

"It isn't enough, sir. I know Jabir."

"Listen, major, you're tired and you and your men are beat up. You need to rest. When all is said and done, we can only do so much. The Afghan president accepts that he's the one making the final call. And, anyway, don't you think it's possible that Jabir is messing with us?"

Exasperated, Connor slammed his fist on the general's desk, scattering the neatly set out line of pens and pencils. "No. The president's the target. I'm sure of it."

Connor had overstepped the mark. The general's expression darkened. "You're dismissed, major. Get some shut-eye. That's an order. It's ten o'clock now. We'll review the latest intel at 1500 hours. The president isn't making his speech until 1900 hours, so there's still time to try to figure out exactly what's going on here."

Connor had been to visit Danny and Ben in the medical centre. They'd been pretty knocked about in the bomb blast, but the docs had given them the all-clear for operations. Now he lay on his bunk in his tent. The stifling heat was almost overwhelming and sweat glistened from every pore of his skin. No way could he sleep, despite being exhausted. Tossing and turning, Jabir's grinning face occupied his thoughts alongside the nightmarish image of the headless corpses of Khalid and Baxter. Over and over, he tried to figure out how Jabir planned to assassinate the Afghan president.

By revealing the target, Jabir would surely realise that no one could get anywhere near the president. A Taliban sniper would either have to be fantastically well hidden or would be too far away to guarantee the shot. Connor pressed his eyes shut and thought about how he would pull off what seemed impossible.

His mind drew a blank. So instead he thought of all the audacious things Jabir Hassani had done in the past. He knew Jabir's career as a Taliban commander had been long and horrifically successful, small raids on ISAF checkpoints being followed by attacks on convoys, FOBs and electricity sub-stations. Finally, Jabir had graduated to major uprisings in towns and cities. Jabir was ambitious. He thought "big", wanting to make the sort of impact that made headlines; that made the world sit up and pay attention.

Think big. Very big. Connor suddenly shot upright. "Of course!"

Up in a flash, he ran across Camp Delta's parade ground and crashed through the door to the Ops Room.

Startled, Lieutenant Sharp jumped in his chair.

"Show me the visuals from our drones. Those covering where the president's going to make his speech near the dam," Connor demanded.

"Of course, major." Sharp tapped on his laptop to bring up the live drone camera feeds. "There you go, sir. Actually, I was just about to come and find you."

"Why?" Connor asked, only half listening. He was squinting at the laptop's split screen, which displayed four real-time camera inputs from two separate drones.

"At about the time of your helo evac in the valley last night, our comms surveillance unit intercepted a mobile phone call originating nearby."

"And?"

"It was to Jabir Hassani. Like to listen to it?"

Connor stopped what he was doing and nodded. Sharp hit another key on his laptop.

"......*They have been deceived. It is enough of a victory for one day. Tomorrow, they shall all die. Well done, Shafiq. Come and join us. We shall watch them die together.*"

A shiver ran down Connor's back. "Don't suppose they got a fix on Jabir's phone's location, did they?"

"Yes. It was to the north. But it's of no use, sir.

He was on the move and the phone was switched off immediately after the call. He could be anywhere by now."

"Damn!" Connor tightened his fist.

Sharp grinned. "But they have managed to track the phone of the sender, the one called Shafiq. He left his phone powered on. He was on the move for three hours. Finally, he stopped here, sir." He flipped screens to show a map. A blinking red dot marked the location.

"They're in the mountains," Connor observed. "About three kilometres from the Dhala dam."

"Yes, major. A splendid panoramic view, I reckon. I've asked that a high-altitude Predator drone is diverted to scan the area."

Connor nodded. "Good. Yes, it all fits... Get General Patterson and everyone else down here. They're going to want to hear this."

"Hear what exactly, sir?"

"That I've figured it out... Jabir's going to blow the dam! And as a wall of water pours down towards Kandahar, Jabir will be watching it sweep away the president and everyone else."

The blood drained from Sharp's face. "B—B—But thousands of people will drown. Maybe tens of thousands. There isn't time to evacuate."

"Then we'd better stop it from happening."

CHAPTER ELEVEN
The shahid

Jabir's camp, Arghandab valley

"Come, Shafiq, sit beside me. It is a momentous day. We shall watch history unfold together."

Jabir was in an excellent mood. Sitting cross-legged on a plump velvet cushion embroidered with gold thread, he popped a grape into his mouth and gazed down into the valley. Far in the distance, he could just make out the Dhala dam. "Ibrahim, bring me a glass of tea and my binoculars."

Shafiq sat down. "Do you think they'll cancel the president's speech?"

"Perhaps, if they are wise. But no matter. The destruction of the dam will proceed and the world will realise that, even after years of war, we Taliban still control our country."

It was six o'clock. The sun was low and cast a rich golden glow over the Arghandab valley. Shafiq sighed and then looked all round. "Where's Father? He will want to watch this too. I haven't seen him all day."

Jabir laughed lightly, reached out and placed a comforting hand on the boy's shoulder. "You should feel proud. Faisal volunteered to lead my men. Your father — my brother — will soon be making the journey to Paradise."

Shafiq frowned. "What do you mean, 'to Paradise'?"

Jabir pointed towards the Dhala dam. "He is there. Hiding in the maintenance tunnels. Watching over the explosives. He will detonate them at exactly seven o'clock. But do not worry, Shafiq. Your father will become a shahid, and will pass first through the gates of Paradise."

Shafiq leaped to his feet. "No! He can't! He mustn't. I don't want him to die."

CHAPTER TWELVE
Dam raid

Inside Dhala dam

The warren of concrete tunnels inside the dam
was lit by fluorescent strip lights. Faisal and
six of Jabir's men had been let in the previous
morning by a maintenance worker sympathetic
to their cause.

Faisal headed for the level three tunnel.
He had been informed that it was perfectly
positioned, about two thirds the way down the
dam — its weakest point if blown from inside.
Faisal directed the men as they stacked the
wooden crates of explosives up against the
wall. He then took great care inserting the
detonator into the priming charge. He ran wires
to a battery pack and checked that the circuit
worked. It was done. A flick of a switch was all
that was needed to detonate a bomb big enough
to punch a massive hole in the dam. He knelt
and led his men in prayer before sending two of
them to guard each end of the tunnel, and the
remaining pair to patrol the level above.

With less than half an hour to go, and having
spent the day reading aloud from his Qur'an,

Faisal readied himself for his journey to Paradise. He shaved off his beard, then pouring water into a small bowl, he washed his face and hands. He was calm, happy and content.

Danny grabbed hold of the handle attached to the heavy reinforced steel door. It was located to one side of the dam, and gave access to the heavy machinery controlling the flow of water through the sluice gates. Beyond the room stairwells led into the structure of the dam, and the network of tunnels. He waited for Connor's signal over the radio. A safe distance away, engineers from bomb disposal readied their equipment. They would enter with a Ranger escort only when Delta Force gave the all clear.

On top of the dam, Connor, Ben and Sam checked their ropes and climbed over the railings. Leaning back and letting the ropes take the strain, Connor issued the order to move, and together they abseiled rapidly down the dam towards an access grille to level four. At the same time, Danny hauled the door open and quietly slipped inside the control room, with Jacko and Sparks close behind.

Connor's boots bounced lightly as he fed metre after metre of rope through his hands and harness. In seconds he'd reached the same height as the grille. It was located close to the sluice gates, where thousands of gallons of water a minute gushed through. It fell to the valley below, feeding the river, canal and irrigation channels. He traversed sideways, skipping over the dam's smooth concrete. He reached out and grabbed one of the grille's bars.

Connor was quickly joined by Ben and Sam. He ignored the spray pounding his face and set about attaching a separate rope to the grille. This would stop it plummeting when removed.

Meanwhile, Danny made his way swiftly through the control room, only pausing briefly to examine the body of a maintenance worker whose throat had been cut. Surrounded by pipework and whirring machinery, the air was filled with the constant muffled roar of fast-flowing water. Jacko and Sparks covered Danny as he hurried to a watertight hatch, which led to level two of the maintenance tunnels and the stairs down.

Using both hands and all his strength, Danny tried to turn the wheel to unlock the hatch. Stubbornly, it refused to budge. Jacko lent a hand. Between them, they finally got it to yield and they hauled the hatch open. Sparks pointed his silenced M4 through the gap and targeted two insurgents walking towards the door. They were midway along the tunnel. Sparks fired four shots, all hitting their mark, and the Taliban collapsed to the floor.

Faisal snatched the cloth away from his face. He thought he'd heard something over the constant muffled roar of water. It sounded like men crying out. He reached for his AK-47 and called out to the men guarding the ends of level three.

"Major," Danny whispered into his throat mic. "The Taliban are still here. Two targets down in level two tunnel. We're proceeding down to level three, over."

"Copy that. We're entering level four, over."

The grille now hung from a rope. Sam clambered into the ventilation shaft, followed by Ben. The main access tunnel was empty. "Clear!"

Connor followed. "Level four clear, Jacko. We're proceeding up to level three via the mid-tunnel access ladder, over."

Faisal was convinced there was a problem, despite his men at either end of level three signalling that all was well. Clutching his rifle he moved over to where an access ladder led to the level below. He leaned forward, peered down and listened. Was that whispering he could hear? Or just water? He glanced at his watch. Ten minutes to go, or, he could blow the dam now. Yes, he thought, blow it now, before it is too late.

CHAPTER THIRTEEN
Take down

At the north end of the dam, Jacko, Danny and Sparks quietly descended the concrete steps. They saw shadows, movement and heard voices speaking Pashto. Without hesitating they advanced, entering level three. A silenced burst of fire from Jacko's M4 killed both guards at close range.

It was only the sound of his men falling down that made Faisal turn. American soldiers were in the tunnel! He fired his AK-47 from the hip. A bullet smacked into Sparks's shoulder and he crumpled to the floor. Jacko dragged him clear of the Taliban's line of fire. Danny tucked in behind some piping as bullets struck the walls around him. "Target located! Major, looks like the action is on level three! Sparks is down."

Danny and Jacko returned fire at the Taliban gunman. The man — Faisal — let out a cry and fell behind a row of crates.

Faisal was wounded and in agony, but he could see the detonation switch. It was almost within reach. He stretched out his hand.

"Danny, cover me, over," Connor said over the comms. He emerged at speed from the access ladder and spotted Faisal reaching up for a box on top of a stack of crates. Connor shot him twice in rapid fire and then sprawled flat against the ground. He'd spotted two more Taliban break cover at the far end of the tunnel. Jacko had them covered and a short burst of fire took them down. Connor rolled to where Faisal lay and quickly checked that the Taliban fighter was dead. He was.

"Secure the tunnel," Connor shouted. "Danny, sitrep, over."

Danny was already applying pressure pads to Sparks's shoulder, while Jacko covered the door they'd entered through. "Sparks needs immediate medevac. He's taken one in the shoulder, sir. Think the bullet's gone right through, over."

"Level three secure, over," declared Sam.

"Good, Sam and Jacko hold positions. Ben assist Danny getting Sparks up top, over."

Danny and Ben hauled Sparks up the stairs, while Connor pressed on ahead. He was in a hurry. He had to confirm the dam was clear, and he had one more job to do.

CHAPTER FOURTEEN
The final strike

Jabir finished his glass of tea and glanced at his watch. It was three minutes to seven. His wait was almost over. He glanced round. Shafiq had wandered off. Jabir rose to his feet and called out to him.

Unable to hold back the tears, Shafiq had hidden among some rocks with his mobile, out of earshot of his uncle. He repeatedly tried to call his father's mobile number. Every time it failed to connect. He suspected the signal couldn't penetrate the thick walls of the dam, and he despaired. He'd not even said goodbye. Maybe he could've persuaded him not to do it, not to martyr himself.

"There you are, Shafiq. What are you doing? What is that you are holding?"

Tears welled up in the boy's eyes again.

Jabir snatched the phone from Shafiq's hand. The Taliban commander cried out, "No!"

Shafiq tried to grab it back.

Jabir took hold of him roughly. He was seething. "What did I tell you? You had to throw this away. They can track mobile phone signals. Allah have mercy, you haven't left it switched on, have you?"

*　　　*　　　*　　　*　　　*　　　*

Pushing past the guys from bomb disposal,
Connor collared a comms sergeant. "Get me
Lieutenant Sharp in the Ops Room at Camp
Delta." Connor's earpiece crackled as the radio
channel switched over. "Sharp, come in. This is
Delta Primary requesting immediate medevac at
our co-ordinates. Area is secure, disposal team is
clear to enter, over."

"Understood, major," Sharp said in Connor's
earpiece.

"The president can go ahead and give his
goddamn speech. Now listen up, lieutenant; are
you still monitoring the Predator drone's live
visual feed on Jabir's location? Over."

"Affirmative, sir. He's not moved. He's still up
on the mountainside, over."

"Then do it! Put in the call for the strike, over."

"Yes, sir. Of course, over."

Connor stood and gazed up at the mountains.
Circling at three thousand metres the missile
targeting system of the unmanned Predator drone
locked onto Jabir's position. Seconds later two
Hellfire missiles launched. Less than a minute
later they struck their target. Connor saw the
flashes and the rising plume of rock and smoke.

"Goodbye, Jabir."

ABOUT THE AUTHOR

Craig lives in the New Forest in southern England — a stone's throw from where secret agents and spies were trained during WWII. He has spent more than ten years researching and writing books inspired by amazing true stories of wartime courage and determination. He's a big fan of gritty action adventures, and the exploits of Special Forces and Special Operations provide a rich seam of material for Craig's stories. As well as *Task Force Delta*, Craig has written five thrilling adventure novels.

GLOSSARY

checkpoint a roadblock where vehicles are checked

GMV Ground Mobility Vehicle: a customised Humvee

IEDs Improvised Explosive Devices, home-made bombs triggered by remote control

intel short for intelligence

ISAF International Security Assistance Force — the NATO-led mission in Afghanistan

medevac short for medical evacuation: used to get injured troops to hospital for treatment

RPG short for rocket-propelled grenade

shrapnel a small piece of debris thrown outwards by an explosion

sitrep short for situation report: an update on the current state of things

wadi a channel for water